PUMPKIN SPICE

Read the first book in the

FRIENDSHIP GARDEN
series:

Book 1: *Green Thumbs-Up!*

And coming soon:

Book 3: *Project Peep*

the FRIENDSHIP garden

PUMPKIN SPICE

by Jenny Meyerhoff
illustrated by Éva Chatelain

ALADDIN
New York   London   Toronto   Sydney   New Delhi

ALADDIN
An imprint of Simon & Schuster Children's Publishing Division
1230 Avenue of the Americas, New York, NY 10020
This Aladdin paperback edition August 2015
Text copyright © 2015 by Simon & Schuster, Inc.
Illustrations copyright © 2015 by Éva Chatelain
Also available in an Aladdin hardcover edition.
All rights reserved, including the right of reproduction in whole or in part in any form.
ALADDIN is a trademark of Simon & Schuster, Inc., and related logo is a registered trademark of Simon & Schuster, Inc.
For information about special discounts for bulk purchases, please contact Simon & Schuster Special Sales at 1-866-506-1949 or business@simonandschuster.com.
The Simon & Schuster Speakers Bureau can bring authors to your live event. For more information or to book an event contact the Simon & Schuster Speakers Bureau at 1-866-248-3049 or visit our website at www.simonspeakers.com.
Book designed by Laura Lyn DiSiena
The text of this book was set in Century Expanded LT Std.
Manufactured in the United States of America 0715 OFF
10 9 8 7 6 5 4 3 2 1
Library of Congress Control Number 2015941237
ISBN 978-1-4814-3910-7 (hc)
ISBN 978-1-4814-3909-1 (pbk)
ISBN 978-1-4814-3912-1 (eBook)

For Emma

CONTENTS

PERFECT PUMPKIN

Reed wrapped both of his arms around the biggest pumpkin in the Friendship Garden.

"Um, Reed," said Anna, as she picked a withered zucchini plant, "I know that some gardeners talk and sing to plants to help them grow, but I've never heard of anyone hugging a plant."

Reed stretched the tips of his fingers just a bit farther until they touched. Then he let go of the pumpkin. "I wasn't hugging it. I was *measuring* it."

"Does measuring a pumpkin help it grow?" asked Kaya as she removed the Popsicle sticks that had labeled all of the garden's plants. It was almost the end of October. Nothing much was growing anymore.

"Don't you guys remember?" Reed pointed to the flyer hanging on the Shoots and Leaves Community Garden bulletin board. "The Windy City Pumpkin Fest is this Sunday, and I want to win the prize for biggest pumpkin."

"*You* want to win?" Kaya asked him accusingly. "You mean *we* want to win!"

Reed's cheeks turned pink. "I mean I want the Friendship Garden to win. Herbert just needs to grow a little bit bigger."

"Herbert?" Kaya scratched her head. "Who names a pumpkin Herbert?"

Anna studied Herbert. He was the biggest and roundest pumpkin in the Friendship Garden's pumpkin patch. As far as Anna was concerned, Herbert was pretty much P-E-R-F-E-C-T.

When Anna had first moved to Chicago from upstate New York, she didn't think she'd ever get to have her own garden again. But then Anna met Kaya and Reed, and the three of them started a gardening club called the Friendship Garden. Mr. Hoffman, their third-grade teacher, was the grown-up in charge, and they grew all their vegetables at Shoots and Leaves, the community garden in their neighborhood.

In Chicago, many people didn't have room for gardens in their backyards. In fact, a lot of people didn't even have backyards, so sometimes empty lots were turned into growing spaces. There, different neighbors had their own plots of land to plant flowers and vegetables.

"What about Mr. Eggers's pumpkins? That one in the corner of his plot looks pretty big." Anna tilted her head toward the front of Shoots and Leaves. Mr. Eggers was an old man with silver curly hair and a bushy mustache. He was trimming back pumpkin vines, but just then he looked up and frowned at the kids in the Friendship Garden.

"His pumpkin isn't round like Herbert. It's much narrower, but a lot taller," Kaya whispered, "and it might be bigger too. It's hard to tell."

"Okay, everyone, time for a break!" Mr. Hoffman set up his three-legged gardening stool and beckoned for the kids to gather around.

Anna followed Kaya and Reed over to Mr. Hoffman. Next to him stood Simone, a fifth grader whose mom, Maria, was the

president of Shoots and Leaves. That meant Maria was in charge of the whole garden.

"You did great work today." Mr. Hoffman pulled a brown clipboard from his backpack. "I think we are right on target for putting the garden to bed for the winter. Why don't all the teams give me a report? Bailey? How about your group?"

"We were in charge of clearing out the broccoli," Bailey said proudly, pointing to a small section at the front of the Friendship Garden. "They were really easy to pull up."

"But there was so much dirt!" said Mackenzie, wrinkling her nose. "Right, Bay?"

Bailey looked back and forth between Mr. Hoffman and Mackenzie. Finally she wrinkled her nose too. "Yeah, tons of dirt."

"It kept spilling on our shoes," said Mackenzie, pointing at the matching pairs of silver-and-white sneakers on her and Bailey's feet. "We *just* got these."

Kaya leaned over to Anna and muttered, her eyes sparkling. "What a surprise! Dirt in a garden."

Anna covered her mouth to hide a little chuckle.

Mr. Hoffman looked over at the broccoli plants. Bailey and Mackenzie had barely pulled any of them. "It's a good idea to wear an old pair of sneakers on gardening days," he said. "Simone, how did your group do today?"

"We cleared out all the tomato plants," Imani, Simone's friend, answered for Simone. She pointed to the center of the garden where the tomato plants once stood. It was completely empty. Anna was impressed. There had been a ton of tomato plants before.

"Anna?" Mr. Hoffman asked. "How about your group?"

"We picked all the little baking pumpkins." Anna pointed to a row of small round pumpkins lined up at the edge of the Friendship Garden. "And we're almost done pulling up what's left of the zucchini."

Reed raised his hand, but blurted his question before Mr. Hoffman could call on him. "We're not picking the jack-o'-lantern pumpkins yet, right? I need to let Herbert grow until Saturday so he can be as big as possible."

"Friday is the last meeting of the Friendship Garden's fall session," Mr. Hoffman said. "We've got to get our old plants out of the ground and cover the garden with mulch to protect the soil throughout the winter. You can leave the big pumpkins for last, but you'll have to pick them on Friday. It's time to put the garden to bed."

"I can't believe garden club is over!" said Kaya.

"Just until the spring," Anna reminded her. "Right, Mr. Hoffman?"

Instead of answering Anna's question, Mr. Hoffman tugged at his bow tie. He always wore a bow tie to school. Today's tie was orange with tiny black bats all over it. Behind her, Anna heard whispering.

"I hope my mom doesn't make me come to garden club in the spring," said Mackenzie. "This is *so* boring."

"Yeah," Bailey agreed, groaning. "So boring."

"My mom only made me come because of *your* mom," Mackenzie added. "Jamie said I should have told my mom no way like she did."

Anna turned around and looked at Bailey and Mackenzie. Along with the girl named Jamie, Bailey and Mackenzie were part of a group that Anna had nicknamed the Outfit-Outfit, because *outfit* is another word for group, and the three girls seemed to care a lot about their clothes. What they didn't seem to care about was gardening, or being nice to anyone at the Friendship Garden. Anna tried to avoid them whenever they came to meetings, just like Mr. Hoffman was trying to avoid her question.

"Mr. Hoffman?" Anna said quietly. "What will happen in the spring?"

"Well, hopefully the Friendship Garden will continue,"

Mr. Hoffman said. "It's just that all the Shoots and Leaves garden members have to pay money to garden here. Maria didn't make us do that this fall because we were taking over an abandoned plot that had already been paid for. But she can't allow us to garden for free in the spring, and I don't know if the school has enough money to pay the fee."

Suddenly goose bumps dotted Anna's arms. "What happens if we can't pay?"

"Don't worry!" announced Reed. "When I win biggest pumpkin, we'll have plenty of money. First prize is one hundred dollars."

Mr. Hoffman nodded. "I hope that happens, but if we continue gardening here, we'll also need to buy our own tools. We can't keep borrowing from the other garden members. Some of them have been complaining that we haven't been taking care of their equipment. Rakes, hoes, and other tools have been left out instead of being put away in the shed. And sometimes they've been put away dirty. Having money won't matter if the other garden members don't want us here."

Anna felt her neck grow warm. She didn't like the idea of the other gardeners being mad at the Friendship Garden. It had taken Anna, Kaya, and Reed so long to persuade Maria to let them have a garden in the first place.

"All right, everyone." Mr. Hoffman stood up. "Parents will be here soon. Let's put everything away!"

Anna picked up her trowel and began to walk over to the hose. On the way, she saw Mackenzie stick muddy tools into the supply shed before she and Bailey headed to the front gate.

"Hey!" Anna chased after them. Even though she usually tried to avoid Mackenzie and Bailey, the Friendship Garden meant too much to her. "Don't forget to clean your tools!"

Bailey started to walk back to the shed, but Mackenzie rolled her eyes. "They're just going to get dirty again tomorrow. Who cares if people complain?"

Bailey stopped, then turned and looked at Anna. "Yeah," she said. "Who cares?"

"I care," said Anna. "I don't want Maria to be sorry she let us have our own garden."

Mackenzie shrugged. "I'm already sorry she let you have it."

Bailey nodded. "I'd do *anything* for it to get canceled."

Anna couldn't believe what they were saying. Maybe *they* didn't want to come to the Friendship Garden, but why would they want to ruin it for everyone else?

Anna left Bailey and Mackenzie by the gate and got their dirty tools from the shed. Then she joined Kaya and Reed by the utility sink and washed them all.

"Herbert better win," she told Reed. "I really want to keep gardening, and we need our own tools!"

Reed nodded his head seriously. "He's

going to! I already told my parents. They are finally going to see *me* win a trophy for a change instead of my brother, Dylan."

Kaya pumped her fist in the air. "You go, Reed!"

Anna looked over at Bailey and Mackenzie waiting for their parents to pick them up. Mackenzie was peering through the gate like a prisoner in a jail cell, but Bailey was staring back at the Friendship Garden. Anna guessed she was thinking mean thoughts.

So Anna tried to think some nice thoughts. She imagined the biggest pumpkin contest, and Reed holding up a giant trophy and one hundred dollars. She pictured it so strongly, she could feel the excitement and happiness swelling in her chest. Herbert just *had* to win!

CHAPTER 2

PUMPKIN OF CHAMPIONS

The next day, when the bell rang at the end of school, Reed, Kaya, and Anna were the only students from their class who weren't in a rush to get home. They were going to the Friendship Garden.

Garden club happened every day after school, but most kids didn't attend all the meetings. To be a member you only had to garden two times per week. Even Mr. Hoffman didn't go to the garden every day. He had parent and grandparent volunteers to help supervise and walk the kids from school to Shoots and Leaves. Since this was the last week of fall garden club, Anna planned to go every single day.

"Today is going to be the best gardening day ever!" Reed said excitedly. "My dad is *finally* going to be our garden volunteer! Neither of my parents has taken a turn yet, but my dad promised to come today. I can't wait for him to see Herbert!"

Kaya finished coloring a picture of a pumpkin and handed it to Reed. She loved to draw. "I made a portrait of Herbert for you."

Reed's smile burst across his face. "It looks just like him! Thanks."

Reed and Kaya began walking to the door, but Anna stayed at her desk. She couldn't stop thinking about what Bailey and Mackenzie had said the day before. A part of Anna hoped that they wouldn't come to the Friendship Garden today. She felt a little guilty, but she couldn't help it.

Anna stood up and shook those feelings away. After all, Reed and Kaya hadn't liked gardening at first, but Anna had shown them how much fun it could be. Maybe she could show Bailey and Mackenzie too. Anna gathered her belongings and followed Reed and Kaya out to the front of the school. The Friendship Garden always met by the flagpole before walking over to Shoots and Leaves. Anna was surprised to see her father and Collin standing there.

"Hi, Anna Banana," said Mr. Fincher. "Hey, kids."

"Where's my dad?" asked Reed, peering around Mr. Fincher. "It was supposed to be his day."

Anna's father wrinkled his forehead. "I'm sorry, buddy. Your father forgot that your brother had debate team tryouts today. He said to tell you that he would try to come on Thursday."

"Oh," said Reed, his shoulders slumping. "Okay."

Anna didn't think he sounded okay. She stepped sideways so she was standing right next to Reed and whispered, "By Thursday Herbert will be even bigger than he is now."

Reed's face brightened. "Yeah, he'll probably be huge on Thursday, right?"

"Ginormous," Kaya agreed.

"He'll be champion-size for sure." Reed nodded. "I can't wait to get a trophy. My parents will have to put up a shelf for it, just like in Dylan's room."

When the rest of the Friendship Gardeners had arrived, Anna's father said, "Okay, crew. Let's walk to the garden!"

Today there were nine gardeners, including her father. Bailey was there, but not Mackenzie. As they walked, Anna heard Bailey huff angrily behind her.

Anna turned around and Bailey frowned at her. "Jamie invited me and Mackenzie to get manicures today, but my mom said I had to go to garden club. Jamie said they are going to get the same color, Pumpkin Spice. I'm going to be the only one with plain fingernails."

Anna didn't know what to say. Bailey wouldn't be the *only* one. Anna had plain fingernails. So did Kaya. But she didn't think that would cheer Bailey up.

And she *did* want to cheer Bailey up. If Bailey was grumpy, she might not take care of the garden tools, and then that might make the other members of Shoots and Leaves wish there was no such thing as the Friendship Garden.

"Do you want to play Eye Spy Superspy?" Anna asked her. Eye Spy Superspy was a game she had invented. Anna liked inventing games. "First one person spies a letter. Then the first person to find something that starts with that letter gets a point and can choose the next letter."

Bailey shrugged. "Okay."

Anna slowed down so that Bailey could catch up.

"G!" Anna called out as they passed a store called YogaLove.

Reed, Kaya, and Bailey scanned the sidewalks. Finally Kaya shouted, "I got it! Gardeners! I spy us." She pointed at their reflections in a shop window.

"Good one," said Reed. He made a silly face at his reflection.

Kaya turned to Bailey. "You can pick the next letter."

Bailey looked up at the Shoots and Leaves Community Garden sign. They were just outside the gate.

"C," said Bailey, walking into the garden.

"Easy!" Reed waggled his arms and waggled his bottom, then pointed at the

Friendship Garden. "Champion pumpkin!"

Anna, Kaya, and Bailey all laughed, and Anna's heart soared. Maybe today was the day Bailey would change her mind about gardening.

As they walked past Mr. Eggers's garden plot, Mr. Eggers scowled and fiddled with his hearing aids.

"All right, everyone," said Anna's father. "Remember to please clean any garden tools you use and put them away in the shed. Also, try not to make too much noise. We don't want to disturb anyone. Now let's get to work!"

Mr. Fincher clapped his hands and grabbed a couple of weeders for Collin and Jax. Simone and Imani started pulling up the old sunflowers.

Anna looked at Bailey. Without Mackenzie, she wasn't part of a group.

"Want to work with us today?" Anna asked, pointing at herself, Kaya, and Reed.

"Um, okay," said Bailey. Then she looked down at her white-and-silver sneakers.

"How about if Reed and Kaya pull the string bean plants and you and I carry them to the wheelbarrow," Anna suggested. "That job is less messy."

Bailey smiled. "That would be great."

While they worked, they talked about the Windy City Pumpkin Fest.

"It's going to be like a carnival," Kaya said. "Only with pump-kins!" She pulled two string bean plants up at the same time, then shook them both side to side like they were maracas. "Oh, yeah!" she sang.

Anna giggled as she took the plants from Kaya and tossed them in the wheelbarrow. "Are you going to go?" she asked Bailey.

Bailey looked at the ground. "I'm not sure," she said. "My mom really wants me to go, but Jamie . . ." Bailey looked away and bit her lip.

Anna didn't understand. If Bailey's mom said it was okay, why would she even think about missing the pumpkin fest? Anna couldn't wait.

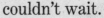

Reed picked an old string bean plant and held it to his mouth like a microphone.

"You should go, go, go

to the pumpkin fest!" he sang. "Where every-one will see that Herbert is the best."

Next Reed pretended his bean plant was a guitar, and Bailey smiled as she took a handful of plants from Kaya and carried them to the wheelbarrow.

"But what about Mr. Eggers's pumpkin?" Bailey asked when she returned. "Don't you think it might be bigger than Herbert?"

Reed stopped playing pretend guitar and squinted hard at Mr. Eggers's garden. "Do you really think so?" His voice sounded small and squeaky.

Anna gave Kaya a worried look.

Bailey's cheeks flushed red, matching the color of her hair. "Maybe the Friend-ship Garden could win something else. Kaya, you're good at art, right? They have a pump-kin decorating contest."

Bailey pointed at the flyer on the bulle-tin board. But Anna looked at Mr. Eggers's garden, not the flyer. His pumpkin looked like it had grown a lot overnight. It wasn't as narrow as before, and it might have got-ten taller too. Anna glanced over at Reed and saw that he was still staring at Mr. Eggers's pumpkin. Then he bent down and wrapped his arms around Herbert. The tips of his fingers touched, and the corners of his mouth turned D-O-W-N.

Anna had never seen her friend look so sad.

CHAPTER 3

MISS PETUNIA PUMPKIN

The next afternoon, only the three original members of the Friendship Garden waited by the flagpole after school: Anna, Kaya, and Reed. Anna didn't know why the other members couldn't come, but she liked gardening with the small group. It almost felt like the Friendship Garden belonged just to them.

Kaya's abuela, Daisy, walked them to Shoots and Leaves. When Anna first met Kaya, she didn't know that the word *abuela* meant grandmother. Now she knew several Spanish words because Daisy often spoke in Spanish.

"So, niños, are you ready for the Windy City Pumpkin Fest?" Daisy asked. "For the moon bounce, face painting, jack-o'-lantern carving, and *muchos* contests?"

"Reed named our best pumpkin Herbert, and he's going to win biggest pumpkin!" Kaya bounced up and down next to Daisy as she walked. "And I'm going to enter the pumpkin decorating contest."

"I think my dad is going to enter the pumpkin bake-off," said Anna. "He's been working on a bunch of different recipes. Chocolate chicken pumpkin puffs and cheesy olive pumpkin waffles are his latest creations."

Kaya wrinkled her nose. "Those sound, um, interesting?"

Daisy nodded. "Your father is an unusual cook. I don't think even you would want to eat those, would you, Señor Reed?"

Reed didn't answer Daisy's question. He just walked alongside the group, staring at the sidewalk. Anna tapped his shoulder, and when Reed turned to her his eyes looked far away, like he'd been lost in a daydream. But his frown made Anna think it wasn't a very good daydream.

Reed blinked. "What?"

"Never mind," Anna said. She figured that Reed was probably thinking about how his parents still hadn't volunteered at the Friendship Garden.

When they arrived, Daisy said, "We only have a few more plants to clear away. That means today we can plant our garlic bulbs!"

"I thought we were done planting," said Anna. "Mr. Hoffman told us it was time to put the garden to bed!"

"That was before," said Daisy as she walked to the Friendship Garden's plot. "Then I explained to him that fall is the time to plant bulbs like garlic and tulips. The bulbs sleep in the soil all winter long and then surprise you in the spring. When they are grown, I will teach you how to make a garlic mojo. *Muy delicioso*."

"Oooh! My dad will want to learn how to make—" Anna started to say, but she was interrupted when Kaya shouted, "Look!"

Kaya pointed at the far end of the garden, to their pumpkin patch.

"But, *chula*, I don't see anything," Daisy said.

"That's the problem! Where's Herbert?" Kaya's eyes searched up and down the garden plot, as if Herbert might have rolled away.

Anna whirled her head to look at the pumpkin vine. Kaya was right! Their three other jack-o'-lantern pumpkins were safe and sound, but Herbert—their biggest, most beautiful pumpkin—was missing. "What happened? Where did he go?"

Anna looked at Reed. He was staring at the spot where Herbert had been, his mouth hanging half open.

"Do you think he was eaten by raccoons?" Kaya asked.

"It's very unlikely, *niña*," said Daisy. "If they had been eating I think we would see some pumpkin left."

"Do you think Mr. Hoffman picked him already?" asked Anna.

Kaya shook her head. "Mr. Hoffman said we could let Herbert grow until Friday. Besides, we just saw Mr. Hoffman at school. Wouldn't

he have told us if he'd picked our pumpkin?"

"Maybe someone else took Herbert," Reed said.

"What do you mean?" Kaya widened her eyes. "Do you think someone stole him?"

"I am sure no one stole the pumpkin," said Daisy. "There is bound to be a simple explanation."

Suddenly Anna remembered Bailey saying that she would do anything to end their garden club. Had *she* taken Herbert so they couldn't pay the fee? Anna couldn't believe it. She thought that Bailey was starting to *like* the Friendship Garden.

Maybe that's why Bailey hadn't come to the garden today. She was probably busy getting rid of Herbert!

"I think I know who took it," Anna said.

"*Dios mio!*" said Daisy. "My goodness. Hold on, *niña*! Our first step is to ask Maria if she knows what happened."

Anna, Kaya, and Reed followed Daisy to the little shed at the front of Shoots and Leaves. They had to pass by Mr. Eggers on the way, and he stared as they walked.

Daisy knocked on the door of the shed, and Maria opened it.

"Hello!" Maria smiled. "How are my favorite young gardeners? Let me guess." Maria looked at Reed. "Are you here for a snack?"

Kaya shook her head. "Maria, something terrible has happened! There's been a crime."

Maria stepped outside and looked around. "What are you talking about?"

"No, no," said Daisy, holding up her hands. "No crime. One of the Friendship Garden's pumpkins has gone missing. We wondered if you knew what happened."

Maria shook her head. "I have no idea. I've been here all day, but I haven't seen anything out of the ordinary."

"It was here yesterday afternoon," said Anna. "I remember because Reed was showing his nanny the pumpkin when my dad and I left."

"What time did you leave?" Kaya asked.

Anna thought for a moment. "Five o'clock," she answered.

"And now it isn't here." Kaya put a finger to her head. "That means it was taken sometime between yesterday at five o'clock and today at three."

"Not at five. Not at three."

Anna looked behind Maria at Mr. Eggers.

He was pointing a finger at Reed as he spoke.

"I saw this young man here yesterday afternoon. We had a nice long chat about pumpkins. I left at five thirty and your pumpkin was still under his care."

Anna looked at Reed and he nodded, but his face looked glum.

Mr. Eggers cleared his throat and continued. "I came here to check on my own Miss Petunia Pumpkin at ten this morning." Mr. Eggers pointed at the tall, narrow pumpkin growing in his garden. "I didn't see any sign of your big pumpkin. But I did see a pair of pruning shears lying in the middle of the path right next to *your* garden." Mr. Eggers shook his finger at Anna. "You kids need to be more careful about leaving tools lying around."

"We didn't leave them there!" Anna had

made sure all the equipment was put away before she went home last night. She was certain of it.

Mr. Eggers turned to Maria. "The shears were lying on the path next to those kids' garden." He wrinkled his nose. "That's not only messy, it's dangerous. What if someone had tripped over them?"

"I'm so sorry, Frank." Maria put her hand over her chest. "I'll make sure their teacher has another talk with them."

"Hmpf." Mr. Eggers frowned. "I'll say it again: these children are too little to handle their own garden."

Maria looked at Anna, Kaya, and Reed sternly. "I'll keep a closer eye on them," Maria said. "Thank you."

Mr. Eggers went back to his garden, where

he began to squirt the pumpkin vines with a spray bottle.

"So your pumpkin's whereabouts are still a mystery," Maria told the kids. "I'll ask around and see if anyone else in the garden knows what happened." She cleared her throat. "In the meantime, I want each of you to check in with me before you leave today. I need to make sure that you don't leave any tools lying around."

"*Gracias*," said Daisy. "*Voy a tener ojos de lince.* I will watch them like a hawk." She led the kids back to the Friendship Garden. "I know it will be hard to think about anything other than your missing pumpkin, but we must get our garlic in the ground today. Are you three ready?"

Reed nodded. "I'm ready."

Anna wanted to look for Herbert, but maybe they could plant quickly and look afterward. "I'm ready too," she said.

"I'm not ready." Kaya frowned and glanced at Mr. Eggers as he brushed a bug off Miss Petunia Pumpkin. "But I'll plant anyway."

"Good." Maria pulled a funny-shaped papery ball out of her bag. Anna thought she'd seen something similar before. She squinted at it closely. It was garlic. Her father had used it when he experimented with garlic pumpkin ice cream. That recipe was *not* a success. Y-U-C-K!

"That's actual garlic," Anna said. "Where are the seeds?"

"Garlic doesn't make seeds," Daisy explained. "This part of the plant is called the bulb. It's not only delicious to eat, it is

 also where next year's plants come from."

Daisy pressed the garlic bulb between her hands, and it broke into several smaller pieces.

"These pieces are called cloves. Inside each clove is a brand-new garlic plant ready to grow." She poked a finger in the soil and dropped the garlic clove down the hole. Then she covered it back up with fresh dirt.

"Plant each clove one and a half inches deep and leave three inches between each one." Daisy pulled several more garlic bulbs from her bag and went to plant in her own garden.

"Do you guys want me to make up a garlic game?" Anna asked.

"How can we play a game?" wailed Kaya. "Aren't you both worried about Herbert?"

Reed shrugged. "I'm sure he's fine."

Anna couldn't believe her ears. *"Fine? What about the contest? The prize?"*

Reed looked at the dirt. "Herbert wouldn't have won anyway."

Anna couldn't believe Reed was giving up on Herbert.

"Well I think Herbert would have won." Kaya lowered her voice to a whisper. "Mr. Eggers probably took him because he realized Herbert was bigger than Miss Petunia Pumpkin. He stole Herbert so that he could win the biggest pumpkin contest."

Reed tilted his head at Kaya. "Come on. Mr. Eggers is a grown-up. He wouldn't steal a pumpkin from a bunch of kids. And sometimes he can be really nice."

"Him? Nice?" Kaya said. "Anyway, how

else would he know that those garden shears were on the path by the Friendship Garden? His plot is way over on the other side. He wouldn't have any reason to be near our garden unless he was stealing our pumpkin."

Anna nodded thoughtfully. "You might be right, but what about Bailey? She could have taken the pumpkin."

"Bailey?" Reed scratched his head.

Kaya looked confused too. "Why would she steal it?"

Anna poked her finger in the soil and popped in a garlic clove. "Bailey wants us to *lose*—not only the contest, but the entire Friendship Garden." Anna explained what Bailey had said about the club being canceled.

"Maybe she thought if the pumpkin went missing," Anna continued, "we couldn't win the contest, and we wouldn't be able to pay the fee for Shoots and Leaves. Then she'd be able to get manicures every day, or whatever those Outfit-Outfit girls like to do."

Kaya folded her arms across her chest and tapped her foot on the ground. "So. We've got two suspects."

"Yep," Anna agreed. "It's a real pumpkin-patch mystery."

CHAPTER 4

PUMPKIN BURGERS

Later that afternoon, Anna and Collin helped their father cook dinner. He was testing two new pumpkin recipes: pumpkin jalapeño burgers and pumpkin potato chips.

"Okay, Collin," said Anna's father, "you are going to be my smusher. Push up your sleeves and wash your hands!"

Mr. Fincher put ground beef and pureed

pumpkin from one of the Friendship Garden's little baking pumpkins into a bowl.

"Anna, I'd like you to be my potato slicer for the chips. Think you can handle it?" asked her dad.

"Sure!" Anna put a potato on the slicer, just like her father showed her. She stuck the holder into the end of the potato, then slid it back and forth. Perfect circles of potato came out the other end.

While she was slicing, Anna told her father and Collin all about their pumpkin patch mystery. "Kaya thinks Mr. Eggers stole Herbert," Anna said, "but I'm pretty sure it was Bailey."

"Whoa there, Banana!" said Mr. Fincher. "It's not right to accuse people without any evidence."

"But, Dad," Anna said, moving the slicer back and forth, "our evidence is that Herbert is missing. He couldn't have gotten up and walked away by himself! What else could have happened?"

"I can think of several other explanations." Mr. Fincher took the potato slices from Anna and put them in a bowl, then he drizzled on some olive oil and pumpkin pie spices. Lifting the bowl to his nose, he closed his eyes and sniffed.

"*Mmm.* I wonder if your mom will want any of my pumpkin recipes for the restaurant."

Anna's mom was the head chef at a fancy new restaurant. Anna's dad had only started cooking when they moved to Chicago two months ago and he became a stay-at-home dad. Now he liked to try new recipes in the kitchen, and most of his food was, well, *different.*

"We should probably taste them first," Anna suggested as she looked at Collin happily smashing hamburger meat and pumpkin together. Truthfully she wasn't too sure about her father's latest recipe invention. But she was S-U-R-E about Herbert.

"We have lots of other evidence," she explained. "For example, Bailey said she'd do *anything* for garden club to be canceled."

"Actually," said Mr. Fincher, "what you are talking about is a theory, an idea. When I say evidence, I mean actual clues. For example, did someone leave a footprint in the dirt when they picked the pumpkin?"

Anna gasped. "We didn't look at the dirt! I bet there *is* a footprint." She had a feeling the footprint would show the sole of a certain sparkly white-and-silver sneaker.

"Maybe." Her father nodded. "But even a footprint won't tell you for sure that the pumpkin was stolen. I bet Herbert turns up tomorrow safe and sound."

"Or," suggested Anna, "tomorrow we will find lots of clues that we didn't notice before. Then Bailey will have to confess."

Mr. Fincher looked at Anna for a long time. "It's very serious to accuse someone of something they didn't do. Promise me you won't go around telling people that Bailey took Herbert."

Anna looked her father right in the eye. "I won't," she said. Then she finished her thought in her head: *Not until the evidence proves that I'm right.*

"Okay," said Mr. Fincher. "Let's get these burgers on the grill."

Mr. Fincher cooked the rest of the dinner while Anna and Collin set the table. But Anna had a hard time concentrating, even when her mom checked in from the restaurant on the computer. She couldn't wait to get back to the garden to find the evidence that would prove her theory. She just knew that Bailey had taken the pumpkin.

That night Anna watered her plants as she got ready for bed. She had three plants: a fern named Fern, a cactus named Spike, and a spider plant named Chloe. When she watered them, Anna usually talked to them too. She'd learned from a TV nature show that talking to plants can help them grow, but talking to plants also helped *her* think.

"It had to be Bailey. Right, Fern?" Anna poured Fern a little water. "But how could Bailey sneak Herbert home? We would have noticed it if she tried to hide him under her jacket or in her backpack."

"Here's how I think it happened," she said to Spike as she gave him a tiny bit of water. Spike never liked his soil to get too wet. "I think Bailey brought her mom to the garden later and pretended she was *allowed* to take the pumpkin."

A shiver of fear ran up her spine. What if Bailey had turned Herbert into a jack-o'-lantern? They wouldn't be able to enter him in the contest!

"I hope I'm wrong," Anna told Chloe. She didn't give Chloe any water because Chloe liked to take a day off between drinks. But she did turn Chloe's pot around so that her other side could look out the window. "I sure hope they didn't have time to carve Herbert yet! We need him to win so we can pay the garden fee!"

Anna set her little red watering can on the sill next to the plants and then climbed into bed. As she waited for her father to tuck her in, Anna thought of all the clues she would find the next day. Then she thought of Reed, who had been so excited to win his very own tro-phy but had now given up. When Anna first moved to Chicago, she didn't have any friends. She really wanted to start a garden but didn't know if anyone would want to garden with her. Then Reed had gone door-to-door to find kids to help start the Friendship Garden.

Now it was Anna's turn to help Reed. She decided then and there that she wouldn't stop looking for the thief until she solved the mystery.

A PUMPKIN POEM

At school the next day, Anna wore tights with pictures of magnifying glasses on them. She called them her detective tights.

Like a good detective, Anna observed Bailey very carefully during morning meeting. That was the time in Mr. Hoffman's classroom when everyone sat in a circle and talked about the daily schedule.

Anna had a hard time listening to Mr. Hoffman. She was too busy looking for clues.

Bailey, Jamie, and Mackenzie sat together across from Anna. Jamie kept whispering things in Mackenzie's ear. Anna wondered if they were whispering about Herbert.

Every time Jamie whispered to Mackenzie,

Bailey would lean closer, but Jamie cupped her hands tightly, like she didn't want Bailey to hear. Anna decided they couldn't be talking about Herbert. It didn't look like Bailey was part of the conversation at all.

Then Anna studied Bailey's hands for clues. Maybe she still had dirt under her fingernails. Anna knew it had been a couple days since Bailey had picked the pumpkin, but she also knew that it could be really hard to get the dirt out from under your fingernails.

But Bailey's fingernails didn't look dirty. They looked orange! Like she had colored them with orange magic marker.

Anna sighed. Finding clues was harder than she'd thought it would be, even with her detective tights.

When morning meeting was over, Mr. Hoffman told his students that they would be writing poems.

"Last week we wrote cinquain poems. Today I have a new form for you to try: haiku. A haiku poem only has three lines. The first line has five syllables, the second line has seven, and the third line goes back to five."

Mr. Hoffman passed everyone a sheet of paper with three lines on it.

"Haiku are typically observations about nature that use sense words to help the reader feel an emotion. Is it a scary thunderstorm? A peaceful sunset? Okay, I'd like everyone to give his or her first haiku a try. Who remembers how to count syllables?"

Anna and a bunch of other students clapped their hands three times as they said *syl-a-bull*, just like Mr. Hoffman had taught them.

"Great," said Mr. Hoffman. "Give it a try. And have fun. Remember, first drafts are supposed to be stinky. It's okay to feel like you are doing it wrong!"

Anna sharpened her pencil and stared at the blank sheet of paper. She didn't want to write a poem—she wanted to figure out what had happened to Herbert. She looked up at the clock. It was only nine thirty. It would be hours and hours until she would be outside in the garden.

Hmm, thought Anna. *Gardens are part of nature*. She wrote a first line.

A missing pumpkin.

That was five syllables. Now she needed a second line.

Where did it go?

That was only four syllables. She needed more.

"When you've got a first draft, raise your hand," said Mr. Hoffman. "I will match you up with a critique partner so you can begin to revise."

Anna tapped the pencil against her chin and tried to think of more words for the second line of her haiku. She already had a title: "Herbert." She wrote it at the top of her paper.

Where did it go? The sky saw.

Anna frowned. The sky did see what happened, but it couldn't help her solve the mystery. Anna finished her poem.

A missing pumpkin.

Where did it go? The sky saw

The orange-fingered thief.

Anna counted her syllables. The last line was tricky. Did orange count as one syllable or two? Anna could pronounce it both ways. But she liked her haiku. Anna raised her hand. When Mr. Hoffman saw, he beckoned her to his desk.

Anna showed him her paper. "It just kind of came out," she explained.

Mr. Hoffman read her poem. He smiled. "Orange-fingered thief," he said. "I like that! It reminds me of that saying about thieves being 'caught red-handed.' But a thief who steals pumpkins would be orange-fingered. Very descriptive."

Anna's chest seemed to glow with pride. It felt good to hear Mr. Hoffman say those things about her words, even though that wasn't what she'd meant. She had been thinking about Bailey and her orange fingernails, but she didn't want to tell Mr. Hoffman that. Her father had been right. She couldn't tell anyone until she had absolute P-R-O-O-F!

"Jamie, come on up," Mr. Hoffman said. Anna turned and saw Jamie walk to the front of the classroom. "You girls can go in the hall and read each other's poems. Remember how you do a critique? First tell your partner one thing you like, then ask them one question about something that isn't clear. Lastly, give one more positive."

Anna nodded, and she and Jamie went into the hall. They sat down next to the drinking fountain and traded papers. Anna read Jamie's haiku.

> Snow falls on my head.
> I spin and sing "Let It Go."
> I am a princess.

When Anna finished reading, she looked up at Jamie. Jamie was also finished.

"Should I go first?" Anna asked.

Jamie nodded.

"Okay. I like how it's about *Frozen*, but you don't say it. I wonder how the snow is falling. Is it gentle or a blizzard? But I like how I can tell you feel happy."

Jamie nodded, then leaned in to whisper. "In your poem, is the orange-fingered thief Bailey?"

Anna swallowed, but she didn't say any-thing. How could Jamie know Anna was writ-ing about Bailey?

"Because she totally came to school with orange marker on her fingers today—which is so weird. It doesn't even match Pumpkin Spice, like mine and Mackenzie's."

Jamie held up her hand so Anna could see the polish on her fingernails. "It's not *our* fault we got manicures without her. I know her mom said she'd take us after garden club was over, but I wanted to go right after school. It looks dumb to have marker on your nails."

Anna swallowed again. She didn't think it was that dumb. She'd colored her fingernails with marker before too. But she didn't want to tell Jamie that. And she didn't want to talk about Bailey stealing the pumpkin either. She had promised her father that she wouldn't accuse Bailey without proof.

Jamie leaned forward and spoke in an eager whisper. "Did Bailey really steal your pumpkin?"

Anna leaned away from her. She didn't want to talk about Bailey with Jamie. "I think you are supposed to start by saying something you like about the poem."

Jamie rolled her eyes. "Fine. I like the way you call Bailey an orange-fingered thief."

Anna's stomach gave a little lurch. She didn't like the way Jamie kept calling Bailey a thief. Even though Anna did think that Bailey took Herbert, it still made her feel funny the way *Jamie* was saying it.

"You know, my root beer lip balm is missing. It wasn't my fault I couldn't give one of them to Bailey. The package only came with two, and I promised Mackenzie she could have one. Maybe Bailey took my lip balm too." Jamie folded her arms across her chest. "I can't believe her!"

"You can't just accuse her of that," Anna said, her heart starting to pound. "You don't have any proof."

Jamie huffed a noisy breath. "Of course I do. She stole your pumpkin! That means she's a thief."

Just then, Mr. Hoffman poked his head out into the hall. "Are you girls almost done?"

"We just finished," Jamie said, standing up.

Anna didn't want to go back into the classroom yet. She felt like she needed to explain something to Jamie. Anna thought Bailey *might* have taken the pumpkin, but she wasn't

100 percent sure. She didn't have any evidence yet. And even if Anna did find evidence that Bailey took Herbert, it wouldn't mean that Bailey stole something else too.

"Good. Come back in." Mr. Hoffman held the door open for Jamie and Anna. "We're going to share our poems."

Anna followed Jamie and Mr. Hoffman back into class. Her stomach was in knots and her throat was so dry she could barely swallow. Jamie sat down at her desk and glared at Bailey.

"Do I have any brave volunteers who would be willing to read their poems to the class?" Mr. Hoffman asked.

Anna looked around the room. No one was raising their hands.

Jamie was whispering something in Mackenzie's ear. When she finished, Mackenzie's eyes went round as marbles and her jaw dropped open. She looked over at Bailey. Then Mackenzie and Jamie covered their mouths and burst into silent giggles. Bailey's cheeks flamed red, and Anna felt her stomach grow H-E-A-V-Y like a giant rock.

Anna wished she could volunteer, but she didn't want anyone else to know about her poem. What if everyone figured out she was writing about Bailey? Anna folded her poem in half and stuck it inside her desk. Maybe Jamie would forget about it by the afternoon.

"Reed?" Mr. Hoffman raised his eyebrows. "Would you mind reading your poem? I really enjoyed it."

Reed's cheeks flushed pink, but he stood up next to his desk and read from his paper.

Sugar-pie pumpkins

Try to grow as big as Big

Max. But they just can't.

"Sugar-pie pumpkins are small pumpkins for baking," Reed explained. "They can never get as big as Big Max pumpkins. Those are for jack-o'-lanterns. All the instructions for how big the pumpkin can get are already in the seed before you plant it. You can't make a little pumpkin get bigger than it's meant to be." Reed sighed.

Anna thought that was really cool. Some seeds barely looked like more than specks, but they had so much going on inside them. Anna raised her hand and Mr. Hoffman called on her.

"I like the part where you said the pumpkins were *trying* to grow. It made me feel like the pumpkins were real. And then I felt sad for them, because no matter how hard they try, they can never be a different kind of pumpkin from what they are."

Reed nodded, then went back to his seat. Anna watched him closely. A row of colored squeezy stress balls sat lined up on his desk. He usually had one in each hand and squeezed them all through school. Sometimes Reed bounced up and down in his seat. But today he sat slumped in his chair, and he rolled the red ball slowly back and forth across his desk. Anna knew he was still really sad about Herbert. She couldn't wait until she solved the mystery!

CHAPTER 6

SECRET PUMPKIN HELPER

After school Anna was surprised to see Mr. Hoffman waiting by the flagpole.

"I thought Reed's dad was helping in the garden today," said Kaya.

"Reed's brother had a basketball game, and Reed decided he wanted to go," Mr. Hoffman explained.

Anna raised her eyebrows at Kaya. They

both knew that Reed never went to Dylan's basketball games. He thought they were B-O-R-I-N-G.

"Maybe he doesn't care about the garden now that Herbert is gone," Kaya whispered to Anna.

"Mr. H!" Simone said as she and Imani jogged over to them. "My mom told me one of our pumpkins disappeared. What happened?"

"I have no idea." Mr. Hoffman shook his head. "Let's hope it's just a misunderstanding."

"Mr. Hoffman," Anna said. "I think today we should search the garden for clues. We didn't really look for them yesterday. There could be a footprint, or somebody might have dropped something."

"Well, we need to get the rest of the plants

pulled, and we need to start spreading mulch over the top of the garden . . ."

Imani wrinkled her nose. "What is *mulch*? I don't like the sound of that word. Is it going to be gross?"

Anna looked at Kaya and giggled. Mulch *was* a funny sounding word.

"Mulch is a mixture that you spread over the top of your soil as a covering. It's like a warm blanket that helps to protect the soil and seeds during the cold winter. It can be made of many different materials, but our mulch is made of shredded wood bark."

"Phew!" Imani wiped the back of her hand across her forehead. "I was worried it was made out of"—she lowered her voice—"manure."

Anna and Kaya giggled again.

"I'd like to pour manure all over the pumpkin thief!" Simone looked angry. "I can't believe someone hopped the fence and took off with our pumpkin in the middle of the night."

"I asked your mom about that, and she told me that's never happened at Shoots and Leaves before," said Mr. Hoffman, shaking his head. "We may never really know what happened."

When they arrived at the Friendship Garden, there was a wheelbarrow full of mulch waiting next to their plot.

"Okay everyone, we are going to spread this mulch with our hands," Mr. Hoffman instructed.

"Our hands?" Imani looked at the wheelbarrow. "What about splinters?"

Mr. Hoffman held one finger up in the air. "Good point! I bought a couple pairs of kid-size gardening gloves. Right now the Friendship Garden only has enough money to buy two pairs, though. We'll have to share. In the meantime, Anna and Kaya, why don't you pick the last of the pumpkins while Simone and Imani spread mulch?"

Anna and Kaya walked over to the pumpkin vine. There were three pumpkins left, but none of them were as perfect as Herbert.

"This is our chance to look for clues!" Anna told Kaya. "Do you notice anything unusual, like footprints or fingerprints?"

Anna and Kaya peered down at the soil. At first Anna didn't see anything out of the ordinary. No footprints, no fingerprints, no buttons that had fallen off of coats.

Then Anna heard Kaya gasp at the same time that she noticed something sparkling in the dirt. It was underneath the big triangular leaves at the end of the twisty, curly vine where Herbert had grown.

"What is this?" Anna asked. She reached down to pick up the sparkly object.

"An earring?" Kaya blinked several times.

"An earring," Anna confirmed. In her hand

she held a dangly purple-and-green crystal earring. But *whose*?

Could it be Bailey's? Anna couldn't remember if Bailey had pierced ears.

Kaya peered at Mr. Eggers. "I guess I was wrong. I'm pretty sure that earring doesn't belong to our grumpy garden neighbor." Then Kaya yelped and grabbed Anna's arm. "Oh no! He's coming over!"

Anna turned around and saw Mr. Eggers plodding right toward them. She looked around to see if any of their tools were lying on the ground. Nope. What was he going to yell at them for this time?

"You kids find your pumpkin yet?" Mr. Eggers asked.

Kaya shook her head and took a sideways step so she was half hidden by Anna. "He's still missing," she squeaked.

"I guess Miss Petunia Pumpkin will win biggest pumpkin," Anna said stiffly. "Congratulations."

Mr. Eggers tilted his head back and laughed. "Biggest pumpkin? Oh no, no, no. She could never win that. She's not the right kind of pumpkin; she didn't come from that kind of seed. The pumpkins that win biggest pumpkin are bigger than you! They come from special giant pumpkin seeds, and grow so big their owners need a forklift to carry them to the festival. I'm entering her in the perfect pumpkin contest. That's for pumpkins that have perfect symmetry, a rich orange color, and overall appeal. I've entered dozens of times, but I've never won before. Biggest pumpkin! Ha!" Mr. Eggers laughed again. "Didn't your boyfriend tell you how it works? I told him all about it the other day, right before your pumpkin went missing."

Kaya made a face. "He's *not* our boyfriend. He's just our friend!"

Anna nodded. "He must have forgotten to tell us because he was trying to figure out what happened to Herbert."

Mr. Eggers made a *tsk, tsk* sound. "Well it's too bad. Your pumpkin could have won the most perfect pumpkin contest. I've been feeding it my special pumpkin fertilizer all summer, you know. Was going to give one final spray the other day, but it was gone."

Anna and Kaya looked at each other with their jaws hanging open. Grumpy old

Mr. Eggers had been helping them? Maybe he wasn't as grumpy as he seemed.

"I figured you kids wouldn't know how to take proper care of a pumpkin." He shook his head. "Kids these days don't know how to take care of *anything*."

Nope. He was still crabby.

Mr. Eggers turned around and shuffled back to his garden.

After he was gone, Anna walked over to the supply shed and took out two things: a pair of pruning shears for cutting the pumpkins off the vine and a weeding fork for digging up the roots.

When she returned to the garden, Anna handed Kaya the shears and she started digging up the pumpkin roots.

"Can you believe it?" Kaya said as she

snipped the first pumpkin stem. "All this time I thought Mr. Eggers took Herbert, but he was actually helping us. Even if he wasn't nice about it, I still feel bad for thinking he was a thief."

Kaya stood up and looked at Mr. Eggers. He was talking to Miss Petunia Pumpkin with a big smile on his face. He wasn't grumpy to pumpkins.

"Maybe I should do something nice for him to say I'm sorry," Kaya said.

"But he wouldn't even know what you were apologizing about!" Anna tilted her weeder back and up popped a clump of pumpkin roots.

"Well maybe I wouldn't apologize," agreed Kaya. "But I could still do something nice for him. I could draw him a portrait of Miss Petunia Pumpkin. Do you think he would like that?"

"Definitely," said Anna. Mr. Eggers thought that anything having to do with Miss Petunia Pumpkin was P-E-R-F-E-C-T.

"I guess that means Bailey is the pumpkin thief!" Anna declared.

"What are you going to do?" asked Kaya. "Tell Mr. Hoffman?"

Anna shrugged. She thought that proving she was right about Bailey would make her feel happy, or maybe even proud. But instead

when she imagined accusing Bailey of stealing Herbert, her stomach felt sour.

"Well, you'd better decide soon," Kaya
said, pointing. "There's Bailey now."

CHAPTER 7

THE PUMPKIN TRAP

Anna looked up at the Shoots and Leaves gate. Bailey was arguing with a woman Anna guessed was Bailey's mother.

Even from far away Anna could see that Bailey's eyes were red and puffy. Her mother gently pushed Bailey toward the garden, but Bailey shook her head.

Mr. Hoffman walked over to Bailey. He bent

down so he was looking right in Bailey's eyes.

Then Mr. Hoffman stood up and led Bailey right to where Anna and Kaya were standing.

Anna's heart ka-thunked like crazy. Her knees began to wobble.

"Anna," Mr. Hoffman said. "Bailey's feeling pretty blue this afternoon. Some other students in our class said that you accused her of stealing Herbert. Is this true?"

A tear trailed down Bailey's freckled cheek, and Anna gulped. It wasn't *exactly* true. She never told Jamie that Bailey stole Herbert. She just sort of wrote it, and Jamie guessed.

But Anna hadn't told Jamie that Bailey *didn't* steal Herbert either.

When Anna looked into Bailey's shiny, sad green eyes, she was almost positive that Bailey wasn't the pumpkin thief. Then Anna looked at Bailey's earlobes. Bailey's ears weren't pierced.

Anna's heart drooped like the wilted old pumpkin vine. Even though she hadn't meant to accuse Bailey without evidence, *she* was the reason Bailey was crying.

"I'm so sorry," she said to Bailey. Anna's voice wobbled as she spoke. "I know you didn't take Herbert. I didn't know it before, but I do now. And I never meant to tell anyone that you were a thief! Jamie

just read my poem and realized that you had orange fingernails. So she thought you were the orange-fingered thief."

Anna pointed at Bailey's fingers, and Bailey curled up her hands and stuck them in her pockets.

"Ah," said Mr. Hoffman. "I see what happened."

He bent down again and looked at Bailey. "It seems like this was an accident and Anna is truly sorry. Do you think you can forgive her?"

Bailey sniffled and looked at Anna through watery eyes. She nodded.

"Okay, I'm going to talk to your mom for a second."

Mr. Hoffman walked away and Anna looked down at her feet.

Bailey sniffled again. "Why did you think I stole the pumpkin? I would *never* steal anything," she said.

Anna looked up at Bailey. "Well, you hate the Friendship Garden. I thought you were trying to stop us from winning the prize so we couldn't pay the garden fee."

Bailey's eyes went wide. "I only said that because Mackenzie hates garden club. I didn't want her to tease me. She's been mean to me lately, so I didn't know what else to do." She paused. "I actually *like* working in the garden."

"You do?" Anna couldn't believe how wrong she was today.

Bailey nodded and wiped her eyes with her sleeve. Then she looked at Kaya. "Did you think I took the pumpkin too?"

Kaya shook her head and shrugged. "I thought it was Mr. Eggers. But it turns out he didn't take the pumpkin either."

Anna looked at their nearly empty pumpkin patch. "I guess we should clear the rest of this out. Will you help us?"

"Just a second." Bailey ran back to the gate and grabbed something from her backpack. At first Anna couldn't tell what it was, but then Bailey sat down and changed her shoes. When

she jogged back to the Friendship Garden she was wearing a pair of old green sneakers.

Anna handed Bailey some pruning shears. "I like your gardening shoes."

"Thanks," Bailey said.

Bailey closed her eyes for a second, like she was thinking hard, then opened them. "Okay, so I have a question. What do you guys think *really* happened to the pumpkin?"

Anna pulled the earring out of her pocket and held it in her cupped hand.

"We found this in the dirt next to where Herbert used to be. We think it might belong to the pumpkin thief. Do you know anyone with these earrings?"

Bailey frowned. "I've never seen them before."

Anna sighed and put the earring back into

her pocket. "The pumpkin festival is only two days away. I think Herbert is gone for good."

"I wish there was something we could do to find him," Bailey said.

"This might be silly," said Kaya, "but when Daisy's cat got lost, we put up flyers everywhere. Maybe we could put up flyers for Herbert. If the person who took him knew how much we missed him, they might give him back."

"That could work," Anna agreed, "but I have another idea too. I'm calling it the Pumpkin Trap. Let's also put up flyers telling everyone we found this earring." She held the earring up so that it dangled. "When the owner calls to get it back, we can ask them if they know anything about Herbert!"

Kaya raised an eyebrow at Anna. "Ooh. Sneaky," she said.

"I like it," said Bailey.

"Do you guys want to come over tomorrow morning to help make the flyers?" Anna asked.

"Sure," Kaya said.

Bailey frowned. "Jamie invited me and Mackenzie over tomorrow to make charm bracelets. She only has two heart charms, though. She told me I have to have the star."

"Oh," said Anna.

Bailey looked at the pumpkins. She looked at Kaya and at Anna, then smiled.

"I don't feel like making bracelets," she said. "I'd rather make flyers."

"Yay!" Kaya and Anna said at the same time.

Then Anna added, "It's time to set the Pumpkin Trap."

CHAPTER 8

PUMPKIN SPICE, PART TWO

The next morning Anna woke up early. She rushed through breakfast and could barely pay attention to TV. Then she sat on the living room couch and watched both the front door and the short hand of the clock as it ticked closer and closer to ten. Just before it got there, the doorbell rang.

"They're here!" Anna called to her parents.

She sprang from her seat and opened the door. Kaya and Bailey stood in the doorway with Bailey's mother.

"Come on," Anna grabbed both of their hands and pulled them inside. "We've got a lot to do."

Bailey's mom laughed. "Sounds like you three are going to be busy. Before I go, I'd like to say hello to one of your parents. Are they around?"

"Right here," said Anna's mom, walking up behind her.

While the moms chatted, Anna and Kaya showed Bailey their fingernails. They were colored with orange magic marker. "To get in a pumpkin-finding mood," Anna explained with a grin.

Bailey gave Anna and Kaya a shy smile.

"Now let's get to work!" Anna exclaimed. "Come on, I have all my art stuff set up already!"

The girls raced down the hallway to Anna's room.

"I can draw a picture of Herbert for our pumpkin flyer," said Kaya. "I remember exactly what he looks like." She grabbed a smelly orange marker and began to draw a round, bumpy shape.

"My dad helped me take a picture of the earring and print it," Anna told them. "Bailey and I will write up the words and then we can make copies."

Bailey took out a blank sheet of paper and wrote FOUND in big letters across the top. At the bottom she wrote:

IF THIS IS YOUR EARRING,
PLEASE GO TO THE SHOOTS
AND LEAVES COMMUNITY
GARDEN AND ASK FOR ANNA,
KAYA, REED, OR BAILEY.

"What do you think?" Bailey asked.

Kaya gave Bailey an orange thumbs-up while she drew a brown stem on top of Herbert. "I like it," said Anna. "Here's what I wrote for the other flyer:

MISSING
ONE PUMPKIN NAMED HERBERT. HIS GROWERS MISS HIM VERY MUCH. IF YOU KNOW WHERE HE IS, WILL YOU PLEASE BRING HIM BACK? THANK YOU!

"Maybe we should offer a reward?" Kaya suggested. "That might help."

"We could give away a free earring." Anna giggled and pointed at the picture on the flyer.

"Maybe we could give away one of the other pumpkins," Bailey suggested. "If someone stole a pumpkin, they probably need a pumpkin. We could do a pumpkin swap."

"Good idea!" Anna added some more words at the bottom of the flyer.

If you bring him back, we
will give you a new pumpkin.

Kaya held up a drawing. "Here's a portrait I drew of Miss Petunia Pumpkin. I'm
going to leave it in Mr. Eggers's garden on
the way home."

Anna thought Kaya's picture was beautiful. She had drawn Miss Petunia Pumpkin sitting on a throne like a queen. "That's great!"

A few minutes later Kaya held up another
drawing. "Here's Herbert."

Anna copied her words onto Kaya's second paper. Then they took the flyers into
the kitchen.

Anna's mom and Bailey's mom were sitting
at the table drinking coffee. Anna's father was
at the oven pulling out steaming trays with

lobster claw oven mitts.

"Mmm," said Bailey. "Those smell good."

Anna sniffed. The air smelled like a mix of cinnamon and other spices, but she had a sinking feeling there was something weird about whatever her father had just baked.

"Would you girls like to try my new recipe?" asked Mr. Fincher.

"Sure!" Bailey stepped up to the counter, but Anna and Kaya looked at each other with worried eyes.

"What did you make?" Anna asked her father.

"Your mother convinced me to try some-thing with more . . . familiar . . . flavors. These are pumpkin spice scones with a cranberry glaze."

"That sounds delicious," said Bailey.

"It really does," said Anna.

"Why don't you girls have a seat and I'll bring you a plate?"

At the table, Mr. Fincher brought them each a golden-brown triangle drizzled with reddish-purple icing. They took a bite.

Kaya closed her eyes as she chewed. "*Mmm.* These are definitely going to win the bake-off."

Anna took a second bite. The scone was flakey, pumpkin-y, and cinnamon-y all at once. The icing was sweet and tart.

"Some people like pumpkin spice on their nails," said Bailey, "but I like it better in my food."

Just then the doorbell rang. "I bet that's Reed!" Anna put down her scone, stood up, and grabbed the flyers. "I can't wait to show him what we did."

Anna, Kaya, and Bailey opened the front door. Reed stood with both hands shoved in his pockets. His nanny was behind him.

"Hi, guys," he said.

"Look what we made!" Anna handed Reed the pumpkin flyer. "We're going to post these up and down the block. I bet the person who took Herbert will feel so guilty, she'll have to bring him back."

"Who's Herbert?" asked Reed's nanny.

Reed didn't answer. He just chewed his bottom lip and kept his eyes on the ground.

"Herbert's our missing pumpkin," Kaya explained. "Show him the other one, Anna."

Anna handed Reed the earring poster next. "We found an earring in the pumpkin patch, right next to Herbert's spot," Anna told him.

Reed's nanny took the flyer. "That's mine! I've been looking all over for it. It must have fallen off the day we picked the big pumpkin, Reedie."

Big pumpkin? Anna couldn't believe her ears. She looked at Reed, but he didn't look back at her.

"So *you* picked Herbert?" Anna asked. "Why didn't you tell us?"

Reed's nanny put her hand on his shoulder. "What are they talking about? You told me every garden club member was allowed to take a pumpkin. This was not true?"

"I don't understand," said Kaya. "You were so excited to enter Herbert in the contest. Why would you steal him?"

Reed's shoulders slumped. He hung his head. "Because I was wrong. Herbert could never win biggest pumpkin. He couldn't even come close. Mr. Eggers told me all about it. Herbert's the wrong kind of pumpkin for that contest. And I didn't want my parents and my brother to see me enter the *losing* pumpkin! I figured if I couldn't enter, then I couldn't lose."

Bailey nodded. "That makes sense," she said.

"You could have told us," said Kaya.

"Yeah," Anna agreed, but when she saw Reed's shoulders sag even further she added, "but we understand why you didn't."

Reed looked up at Anna, Kaya, and Bailey. "I'm sorry I didn't tell you it was me," he said.

"We forgive you," said Kaya. Anna and Bailey nodded in agreement.

"But what did you do with Herbert? Did you carve him?" Anna asked.

"I let Rina give him to her nephew. He's never carved a pumpkin before."

Rina, Reed's nanny, made a sad face. "I took it to him last night. But if I had known all this"—she waved her hand at the flyers—"I would not have told him to carve it up."

"Oh," said Anna. "That's okay. We still have three other pumpkins. Kaya's decorating one. Mr. Hoffman's keeping one for the school, so we can enter the third in the Perfect Pumpkin competition. You guys are all coming tomorrow, right?"

"I'll be there with bells on," said Bailey.

"I'll be there with pumpkins on," said Kaya.

"I'll be there," said Reed. "My whole family's going."

"Great!" said Anna. "And with all the contests we are entering, maybe there's still a chance we can win a prize."

CHAPTER 9

PRIZEWINNING PUMPKINS

The Windy City Pumpkin Fest was already crowded, even though Anna and her parents made sure to arrive right on time. Anna wore her pumpkin tights, of course. There was so much going on she didn't know where to look first: a jumbo pumpkin moon bounce, a pumpkin face-painting booth, and a giant pile of pumpkins for sale. Around the edges of the park were booths for all the contests: the pie-eating contest, the pumpkin bake-off, best-decorated pumpkin, the biggest pumpkin, and the perfect pumpkin.

"What should we do first?" Anna's mom asked.

Anna's father held his tray tightly as several people bumped past him on their way into the festival. "I think I should drop these at the bake-off tent."

"I want to do the moon bounce," said Collin.

"Okay," said Anna's mom. "I'll take you. Let's meet at the biggest pumpkin tent in thirty minutes."

"I'll help Dad bring his scones over to the bake-off," said Anna.

When they arrived at the booth, Anna's father set the tray of scones at the end of the row. Then they looked at all the other entries. Pumpkin bread. Pumpkin chocolate chip cookies. Pumpkin muffins. Everything was made with pumpkin and everything looked delicious.

"I don't know, Banana, this may be tougher than I thought," said Mr. Fincher.

"Don't worry," Anna assured him. "Yours were super tasty. Let's go look at the other booths."

At the pumpkin decorating booth, Anna found Kaya and her parents. Kaya had painted her pumpkin with drips of paint in all different colors. It looked like a rainbow had melted on her pumpkin.

"It's beautiful!" Anna told her.

"But look at all these others!" Kaya exclaimed. "I've never seen pumpkins that look like this."

There was a pumpkin that looked like a hamburger, and another one that looked like a basketball. There was a Frankenpumpkin, a mummy pumpkin, and a vampumpkin. There were three pumpkin witches and a pumpkin owl.

"I didn't know it was supposed to look like *something*." Kaya wrinkled her forehead. "I just did a design."

"Yours is unique," Anna told her. "In a good way, like my dad's scones. I love it!"

Anna and Kaya walked to the next booth together. There they found Mr. Eggers setting Miss Petunia Pumpkin on a little purple cushion.

"Did you ever find your pumpkin?" Mr. Eggers asked.

Anna shook her head.

"That's a real pity. You had a special pumpkin there."

Anna was about to tell him that they were going to enter one of their other pumpkins when she heard a voice calling out behind her.

"Where should I put this guy?"

Anna turned around and saw Reed carrying a big round pumpkin. A man walked next to him with a huge smile across his face. Anna wondered if he was Reed's dad.

"Is that—" Kaya began.

"That looks like Herbert." Anna wrinkled her brow and stared closer at the pumpkin.

"It is!" said Reed happily. "Rina called her sister and her nephew hadn't carved him yet, so she got him back."

"That's great!" said Anna.

"Hi, guys!" Bailey ran over to the perfect

pumpkin booth. She'd obviously just been to the face-painting booth because she had a happy jack-o'-lantern painted on her cheek.

Reed's father set Herbert on the table next to Miss Petunia Pumpkin.

"Your son has a real knack for growing pumpkins," Mr. Eggers said. "He's a natural."

"Is that so?" asked Mr. Madigan, ruffling Reed's hair.

Anna, Kaya, Reed, and Bailey explored the Pumpkin Fest together. They went on the moon bounce, ate pumpkin doughnuts, and watched the biggest pumpkin weigh-off. The winner weighed over seven hundred pounds! It wasn't too pretty, but it was G-I-G-A-N-T-I-C!

Finally another announcement came over the loudspeaker. The judges had chosen the other contest winners. Each winner would see a blue ribbon sitting next to their entry.

Anna, Kaya, Reed, and Bailey raced back to the booths. Anna saw her father standing next to his scones—which had a red ribbon for second place. He picked it up and pinned it to the pocket of his shirt. At the pumpkin decorating tent, the hamburger pumpkin got the blue ribbon and the Frankenpumpkin got the red.

"That's okay," said Kaya. "I still like the way I decorated my pumpkin, and now I have lots of ideas for next year."

Anna could see Reed peering through the crowd, trying to get a glimpse of the perfect pumpkin table, but there were too many people. It was impossible to tell what had happened from so far away.

"Let's go see!" Anna said, and they all took off running.

But when they were halfway there they could see Mr. Eggers holding a blue ribbon high in the air, dancing around in a circle.

Reed stopped. Anna could see the disappointment on his face.

"Come on," she said. "Maybe you got the red ribbon."

When they arrived at the table, Anna couldn't believe her eyes. Sitting next to Herbert was a bright blue ribbon.

She looked at Mr. Eggers. Had she imagined his ribbon?

No. He was holding a blue ribbon too!

"We tied!" he told them. Then he grabbed Anna's and Reed's hands and did another little dance.

"Congratulations to the Friendship Garden!" Mr. Hoffman pushed through the crowd and high-fived his students. "What a great end to our first growing season. Now we can have a second season as well!"

"Ahem," said Mr. Eggers. "I'd like to donate my prize money to the Friendship Garden. You kids really ought to have your own tools."

"Thank you!" they all said at once.

"Don't thank me too much," he said. "I'm still keeping my ribbon." He pinned it to his shirt. "And I'm keeping this." Mr. Eggers pulled a folded piece of paper from his back pocket. When he unfolded it, Anna saw Kaya's beautiful drawing of Miss Petunia Pumpkin.

"I vote that Reed

gets to keep our ribbon," said Anna. "He spent the most time taking care of Herbert."

Everyone agreed that Reed should keep the ribbon, and they also agreed that Herbert could go back to Rina's nephew now that the contest was over.

At the end of the day, Anna's family picked two pumpkins from the pumpkin pile and pulled them home in a wagon.

"That was my most pumpkin-y day ever," said Collin.

"I won my first prize for cooking," said Anna's father, patting the ribbon on his chest.

"I think your reward is that *I'll* cook dinner tonight," said Anna's mother.

"I just have one request," said Anna's father, looking back at their wagon. "Nothing with pumpkin. I'm all pumpkin-ed out."

Anna's mother laughed. "How about you, Anna Banana? Are you pumpkin-ed out?"

"Well," said Anna, "I might not be in the mood to *eat* any more pumpkin, but I could definitely *carve* one."

"Going to a pumpkin festival, winning a pumpkin prize, and then carving a pumpkin all in one day? Are you sure you can handle it?" Mr. Fincher asked.

Anna nodded. She could handle it. It was a pumpkin-perfect day.

ACTIVITY: **GROW YOUR OWN BULBS! (INDOORS!)**

Garlic is a plant that grows from a bulb, but it's not the only one. Paperwhites are a flower that come from a bulb and are easy to grow inside.

What you will need:

One paperwhite bulb (can be purchased
   at a garden or home store)
Marbles or pebbles
Clear drinking glass

What you will do:

First, fill the glass halfway with marbles or pebbles. (If you are using pebbles, make sure they are clean.)

Place your paperwhite bulb, root side down, in the marbles so that half of the bulb is covered and half of the bulb is sticking out on top.

Pour water into the glass until the water is just barely touching the very bottom of the bulb. (Be careful not to splash water onto the top of the bulb.)

Now put your bulbs on a windowsill and wait.

What you will see:

Within a few days, roots should start spreading out from the bottom of the bulb. They will twist and wind their way through the marbles.

Next, little green shoots will sprout up from the top of the bulb, and before you know it, you will have a beautiful white flower.

RECIPE: **MR. FINCHER'S PUMPKIN SPICE SCONES WITH CRANBERRY GLAZE**

Scone ingredients:

2½ cups flour

½ tsp. baking soda

2 tsp. baking powder

½ tsp. salt

½ cup sugar

1 tsp. pumpkin pie spice

½ cup cold butter

1 cup pumpkin puree

⅔ cup buttermilk

Scone instructions:

- Add dry ingredients and mix well.
- Cut in the butter with with a pastry blender until the mix resembles peas.

- Add pumpkin and milk.

- Stir until combined.

- Turn dough out onto a floured surface.

- Form a 9" circle.

- Cut circle into 8 pie-shaped pieces.

- Separate the pieces so they don't touch and place on a greased cookie sheet.

- Bake for 22–28 minutes.

Glaze ingredients:

2 cups powdered sugar

2 tbsp. butter, melted

3 tbsp. cranberry juice

Glaze instructions:

While the scones are baking, mix together all ingredients until smooth, then drizzle over the scones after they have cooled.

Read on for more
FRIENDSHIP GARDEN
adventures in *Project Peep!*

Anna Fincher was trying to pay attention to her teacher, Mr. Hoffman, but she was having a hard time. It wasn't because he was being boring. In fact, he was telling her third-grade class about a party!

For the past two months, Anna's class had watched chicken eggs develop in an incubator. Then they'd seen the eggs hatch, and they'd taken care of the baby chicks as they grew.

"Friday will be our last day with the chicks in our classroom," Mr. Hoffman told his students. "We will have a party to say good-bye."

All of Anna's classmates groaned. Anna

groaned too, but not because of the chicks. She had something else on her mind: Kaya's birthday. She didn't have time to worry about chicks when she needed to be thinking of a present.

In just one week, Anna's friend Kaya would be turning nine years old, and Anna wanted to get her the best birthday present E-V-E-R. That was the problem. Anna didn't know what Kaya would want most of all.

New gel pens? Kaya loved to draw and paint.

Rainbow tights? Anna was wearing tights with suns and moons on them.

Maybe she should get Kaya a squirting bow tie? No, that would be a better present for their friend Reed. He loved practical jokes.

"I'm so sad," Kaya whispered to Anna.

"How will we survive without seeing Banana, Chicken Little, Fluff, and Feather? They're my friends, and now they are going to be gone." She sighed. "Forever!"

Anna nodded. She knew what it was like to say good-bye to friends. When she lived in Rosendale, New York, she'd had two best friends, Haley and Lauren. But since Anna had moved to Chicago eight months ago, they hadn't kept in touch the way she'd thought they would. Even though Anna still wore the purple BFF bracelet they'd made, Anna wasn't sure they still counted as *best* friends.

And if they didn't, then Anna didn't have a best friend anymore.

Kaya tapped Anna's shoulder. "You know what the worst part is? I have to say good-bye on my birthday."

"That's the opposite of a birthday present." Anna frowned. "It's a birthday punishment."

Anna really *did* know the perfect present for Kaya. She just couldn't get it for her. Kaya wanted a pet more than anything.